Pathways to Ancestor

PRAISE FOR *STORYSHARES*

"One of the brightest innovators and game-changers in the education industry."
– Forbes

"Your success in applying research-validated practices to promote literacy serves as a valuable model for other organizations seeking to create evidence-based literacy programs."

- Library of Congress

"We need powerful social and educational innovation, and Storyshares is breaking new ground. The organization addresses critical problems facing our students and teachers. I am excited about the strategies it brings to the collective work of making sure every student has an equal chance in life."
– Teach For America

"Around the world, this is one of the up-and-coming trailblazers changing the landscape of literacy and education."
- International Literacy Association

"It's the perfect idea. There's really nothing like this. I mean wow, this will be a wonderful experience for young people."   - Andrea Davis Pinkney, Executive Director, Scholastic

"Reading for meaning opens opportunities for a lifetime of learning. Providing emerging readers with engaging texts that are designed to offer both challenges and support for each individual will improve their lives for years to come. Storyshares is a wonderful start."
- David Rose, Co-founder of CAST & UDL

Pathways to Ancestors

M.R. Cain

STORYSHARES

Story Share, Inc.
New York. Boston. Philadelphia.

Storyshares
Story Share, Inc.
24 N. Bryn Mawr Avenue #340
Bryn Mawr, PA 19010-3304
www.storyshares.org

Inspiring reading with a new kind of book.

Interest Level: High School
Grade Level Equivalent: 2.6

9781642615241

Book design by Storyshares

Printed in the United States of America

Storyshares Presents

1

Jessie Lascaux parked her pickup truck in the shade of a great spruce. She turned off the car, and the sound of the engine died down. She remained still for a few moments, soaking in the sudden silence.

In the mirror, she could see the bluish sheen of her black hair. Her eyes were gray. People often told her there was something eagle-like about her face.

She didn't lock the truck as she exited. There was never anyone here. She followed the road to the cemetery at the top of the hill. The graves were overgrown with weeds.

She found the graves she was looking for and cleared the weeds off. In the summer heat, Jessie wiped the sweat off her face with the sleeve of her shirt. Then she lit a candle and put wild roses on the graves.

She knew most of the graves well. They were her ancestors: a long line of English, French, and Native names. Yet there were two gravestones at the very beginning of the line she knew nothing about. The date was worn away by the weather, but the names were still readable: Kimi and Pierre Lascaux.

2

Kimi advanced through the bushes, an antique rifle in her hands. She moved soundlessly in her leather clothes. Mere moments had passed since she heard the first screams. She spotted a meadow through the dark trees. Far below, the river rushed past.

In the middle of the sunlit meadow, two shapes struggled. One shape was black, stocky, and covered with fur. It was grunting and growling. The other shape was bright, tall, and slender. It was a man! And he was screaming.

Kimi didn't want to shoot the man, so she aimed wide on purpose. There was a loud crack, and smoke erupted from the gun's barrel. The bear recoiled in terror and ran for the trees. She took aim once more, but the animal was too fast.

Her ears were ringing. Her nostrils were filled with the scent of gunpowder. The man was lying on the grass, groaning softly. One of his trouser legs was black with blood.

Kimi realized he was wearing jeans, boots, and a light blue shirt. The importance of what she had done suddenly overwhelmed her. The man's face was pale and freckled. His eyes were gray. She had saved a white man. A murderer. An enemy.

Fortunately, there was no time to think. The man was bleeding out rapidly. Thinking would have to wait. Kimi grabbed his leg above the knee and pressed down. The man screamed loudly. She wrapped his leg tightly with a scarf.

Beads of sweat appeared on his forehead. Nevertheless, he said, "Thank you."

Kimi knew some English, but the way this man spoke it was different.

"Your name?" she asked.

"Pierre," the man said. The "r" sounds came from the back of his throat.

"I'm Kimi. Here, grab my hand."

She helped him to his feet.

"Oof," she groaned. The man was two heads taller than Kimi and very heavy. She put his arm around her neck and helped him limp toward the trees.

"No," he said. "The other way."

"Where is your camp?" she asked. "I can't go there. They'll do horrible things to me. Kill me."

"No," he replied. "No camp. Boat. The river... It was too fast. I crash there," he explains in broken English. "The men leave me there. They take my things. They say if I come by foot then they return things. I know they lie. I hear them talk. They call me 'French bastard.'

"There was a war in the old country. So they don't like me. Even here. So no new life for Pierre. No new start. The French kill the English families. Or maybe the reverse. So now they hate, forever."

Kimi understood only half of his mumblings. She knew who the French and English were. But war in the old country? She didn't know what he was talking about.

It was clear that he had no place to return to, and his leg was in bad shape. He wouldn't make it far. She did the only thing she could think of: she took him home.

"And the bear?" she asked as they staggered through the woods.

"I come from the river, and I come upon the bear. I think the bear is surprised and frightened, like me. I hope it runs, but instead it attacks. The claws, they cut me, but I fight. And then I hear a shot."

They made it to a small clearing in the hills. There were two huts in the clearing. The rest of the tribe had already migrated into the mountains, ever since the white trappers and miners had begun to move into the region. Kimi's grandfather, Mingan, was too old to make the journey. She stayed with him. Years ago, he taught her how to hunt and forage. Now she provided for both of them.

"What did you do?" Mingan asked as they approached, his eyes wide with fear. There was an axe in his hand.

"Nothing," Kimi replied. They spoke in their native tongue, and Pierre couldn't understand them. "He was attacked by a bear."

"What have I told you a hundred times? If you see a white demon, you run in the opposite direction as fast as you can."

And yet he helped her gently lay Pierre down on the ground.

"Do what you want with him," Kimi said angrily. "If he is so bad, you will have no problem disposing of him."

She turned her back and stormed off. She didn't know if she was angrier with herself or with Mingan. She should have let the bear finish him off, she thought. Then neither she nor Mingan would have to kill him.

3

The white man went through a bad fever. He tossed and turned in fevered dreams. He cried in an unknown language. Mingan anxiously watched his trembling body. Mingan waited for the fever to kill the white man. But instead, the white man got better.

"We cannot kill him," he told Kimi on the third day. "The spirits saw fit to put him in your care. We will help the demon and pray that he does not harm us."

Kimi smiled. In the evening, Pierre was well enough to drink some soup. Within a week, he was cheerful again. He sang loudly in French and limped from tree to tree. He tried to help Mingan, who watched him with fear and mistrust. To Pierre's delight, Kimi taught him some native words.

"What is he doing?" Mingan complained to Kimi. "He should be building a canoe to get back to where he came from. Instead, he chose to stay here and annoy me."

"I don't think he has anywhere to go," Kimi replied. "I think he is trying to help because he is ashamed of being a burden."

In two weeks, the man's leg was nearly healed.

"I think I can make the trip back now," he said to Kimi in a mixture of English and her native tongue. Kimi looked into his serious, gray eyes and saw that he meant it. The next morning, she rose early and helped him prepare for his trip.

As the sun rose, Pierre turned toward them once more.

"Thank you," he said. "You are friends to Pierre more than you know. You help me more than anyone in the white man's world. I never forget it."

As he turned to leave, Mingan suddenly collapsed.

"There is a terrible weakness in my body," Mingan said, gasping.

Pierre threw off his pack and raced back to help Kimi. Together, they carried Mingan into the hut.

In the following days, it became clear that there was no way Pierre could leave. One side of Mingan's body was paralyzed. Pierre, now almost well, was a strong man and could carry Mingan around easily.

"I am healed now," he told Kimi. "I will make traps. You will see, Pierre is a good trapper. Lots of food and fur."

"He is right," Mingan said. He spoke with difficulty. "We need him now. He needs to repay his debt. You helped him before, and now he can help us," Mingan told Kimi.

Kimi noticed that Mingan did not call Pierre a demon anymore.

4

After Pierre's leg healed, he cut down some trees in the forest and built a simple log cabin. He filled the holes with moss, and the cabin became a dry, warm place.

"The white man is crazy," Mingan said, shaking his head. But when the great rains came, Mingan let himself be carried inside without protest.

A month later, Mingan died. Pierre found the cabin empty one morning. It seemed strange to him, since Mingan could not walk on his own. Kimi found Mingan sitting cross-legged beneath a tall spruce tree. Mingan's face was calm. He was dead.

Kimi did not cry. Pierre dug a deep grave in a meadow, and Kimi rolled Mingan's body into a large strip of bark. They put Mingan's bow into the grave with him. Then Pierre filled the grave with dirt. Kimi sang the burial song, while Pierre stood respectfully to the side.

"Will you travel to the mountains to find your people now? There is nothing keeping you here," Pierre said the next day.

"I don't know yet," Kimi replied. "I need some time to think."

5

One day, Kimi and Pierre were preparing an animal skin together. Kimi asked, "What does your name mean?"

Pierre seemed confused. "What do you mean?"

"Well, all names mean something. For example, Kimi means 'a secret.'"

The white man laughed. "You got me there. My name does mean something: 'a rock.'"

She considered his gray eyes. "It is fitting," she said.

A look of panic suddenly appeared on her face. "Listen!"

Pierre kept very still. "I don't hear anything," he said.

"White men are coming," she whispered.

Pierre now heard the voices, too. "They must be coming from the river," he said.

She grabbed the rifle, but Pierre said, "Don't attack them. It will end badly. Kick down your hut and hide in the cabin. I'll take care of it...somehow."

In the cabin, Kimi ducked behind the chair and aimed her rifle at the door. She didn't know what was going to happen. Pierre had helped her before, but Mingan would say that you can never fully trust a white demon. She didn't know who might be coming through that door. It might be strangers, Pierre, or the strangers and Pierre together. The thought horrified her.

Holding the axe in his right hand, Pierre faced the men. There were three of them, each armed with a rifle. They eyed the skin and the tools left on the ground.

"I'll be damned," one of them said in English. He was wearing a European-style hat.

"Why are you here?" Pierre asked. He made no effort to hide the displeasure in his voice.

"One might ask you the same thing," the man replied.

"Aren't you going to invite us in, man?" the second man asked. He was sunburnt and red-faced.

"No. People like you scare away animals. And then I go hungry," said Pierre.

"You are a trapper?"

"Yes," Pierre replied, pointing to the skin with the axe.

"Having any luck?"

"Not much."

"No mining here, huh?" the man with the hat remarked.

"No. Further up river," Pierre replied. "Please, go now."

"Well, alright," the man with the hat replied. "But you best be careful. I heard there's a camp full of savages somewhere around here."

"They all gone a long time now. Killed off."

"You sure?" the third man asked. "I have never seen such skinning tools before."

"I make them myself. Go on now. Don't spoil my luck."

The man with the hat threw up his hands in surrender. As they left, Pierre followed them silently through the brush. He could hardly see them through the thicket, but their voices carried well.

"What a wild man," one of them said.

"He must have gone insane with loneliness. I am sure no one would miss him."

"He's more trouble than he's worth," the man with the hat said. "Did you see his clothes? They were in tatters. He has nothing."

Pierre breathed a sigh of relief and walked back to the cabin. He knocked on the door carefully. He didn't want to get his head blown off. He was certain that Kimi was far more dangerous with the rifle than he could ever be.

"It's me," he yelled.

"Are you alone?" she asked.

"Yes," he replied and pushed the door open. He was staring straight into the barrels of Kimi's rifle. She lowered it slowly.

"Can you be sure they won't be back?" she asked.

"Yes. They think I have nothing worth taking."

"I heard what you told them out there," she said.

"I'm glad," he said. There was a hint of bitterness in his voice. "I know you don't trust me. But I understand."

Kimi grabbed Pierre's hand. The sudden warmth of her fingers startled him.

"Your people will never accept me," he said softly.

"Maybe not," she replied. "But I will."

Silently, they watched the sun journey across the sky.

6

Looking at the gravestone, Jessie realized the answer could lie there. The answer to the fact that she never felt like she belonged anywhere.

"Time is trying to erase all of our names," she thought to herself. "The only thing that can stop it is my persistence. Persistence to ask, persistence to find out."

She had never bothered to learn anything about Kimi and Pierre Lascaux, but this was all going to change. Someone somewhere had to know about them. All that was needed was her effort. She would find their stories, and she would find herself.

About The Author

M.R. Cain is a European writer. He is the author of several novels in multiple languages, including the historical novel The Wolf. Currently, he is living in the Balkans. He loves writing in seedy cafés and watching boxing shows with a cold pint in his hand.

About The Publisher

Story Shares is a nonprofit focused on supporting the millions of teens and adults who struggle with reading by creating a new shelf in the library specifically for them. The ever-growing collection features content that is compelling and culturally relevant for teens and adults, yet still readable at a range of lower reading levels.

Story Shares generates content by engaging deeply with writers, bringing together a community to create this new kind of book. With more intriguing and approachable stories to choose from, the teens and adults who have fallen behind are improving their skills and beginning to discover the joy of reading. For more information, visit storyshares.org.

Easy to Read. Hard to Put Down.

www.ingramcontent.com/pod-product-compliance
Lightning Source LLC
Chambersburg PA
CBHW071230170626
46809CB00005BA/2009